THE DIVIDED FAMILY

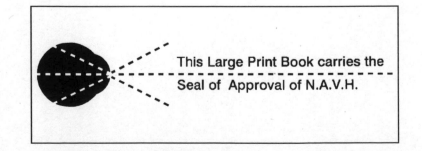

This Large Print Book carries the
Seal of Approval of N.A.V.H.

THE AMISH MILLIONAIRE, BOOK 5

THE DIVIDED FAMILY

WANDA E. BRUNSTETTER
& JEAN BRUNSTETTER

THORNDIKE PRESS
A part of Gale, Cengage Learning

GALE
CENGAGE Learning·

Farmington Hills, Mich • San Francisco • New York • Waterville, Maine
Meriden, Conn • Mason, Ohio • Chicago

GALE
CENGAGE Learning®

LIBRARY OF CONGRESS CATALOGING-IN-PUBLICATION DATA

Names: Brunstetter, Wanda E., author. | Brunstetter, Jean, author.
Title: The divided family / by Wanda E. Brunstetter & Jean Brunstetter.
Description: Waterville, Maine : Thorndike Press, 2016. | Series: The Amish millionaire ; #5 | Series: Thorndike Press large print Christian fiction
Identifiers: LCCN 2016022072 | ISBN 9781410488015 (hardcover) | ISBN 1410488012 (hardcover)
Subjects: LCSH: Amish—Fiction. | Large type books. | GSAFD: Love stories. | Christian fiction.
Classification: LCC PS3602.R864 D58 2016 | DDC 813/.6—dc23
LC record available at https://lccn.loc.gov/2016022072

Published in 2016 by arrangement with Barbour Publishing, Inc.

Printed in Mexico
1 2 3 4 5 6 7 20 19 18 17 16

THE DIVIDED FAMILY

CHAPTER 1

Dover, Ohio

Elsie stood trembling at the foot of her sister's hospital bed, listening to the doctor give Doris and her husband distressing news. In addition to a broken leg, plus a nasty bump on the head, the fall Doris took down the stairs earlier this evening had caused her to miscarry. It wasn't fair. The broken leg would heal, but Doris and Brian had waited a long time for her to become pregnant. The joy they'd felt over the pregnancy, which Doris had seen as a miracle, disappeared before their eyes, like a glass of ice melting on a hot summer day.

Elsie glanced at Arlene, standing beside her with tears trickling down her cheeks. She, too, felt their sister's pain.

When Doris had been taken by ambulance to Union Hospital, Brian rode along. Elsie and Arlene had hired a driver to take them, leaving their husbands at home with the children. Right now, and for many days ahead, Doris would need her family's help and support.

It hurt Elsie to hear her sister's anguished cries after the doctor left the room. Brian took the news hard as well, yet seemed unable to offer

Doris the comfort she needed. Even if sometime in the future Doris got pregnant again, she might never get over her loss.

Elsie and Arlene moved to the other side of the bed, across from Brian. Elsie reached out to clasp her sister's cold hand. "I'm so sorry. . . ." The words nearly stuck in her throat as she swallowed around the lump that seemed to be lodged there.

"I'm sorry, too." Arlene placed her hand on Doris's trembling shoulder. "Elsie and I will do everything we can to help you get through this."

Doris just closed her eyes and continued to weep.

Brian looked up at Elsie with a

distant stare. "Would you mind leaving us alone for a while?"

Elsie slowly nodded. Her body felt heavy as she let go of Doris's hand. As much as she wanted to remain at her sister's bedside, she understood Brian's request to be alone with his wife. This tragedy was something the two of them needed to deal with together. At least for the time being. Hopefully Doris would eventually be more receptive to their sympathy.

"We'll be in the waiting room if you need us." Arlene turned toward the door, and Elsie followed. They took seats in the waiting room down the hall.

Dabbing at her tears, Arlene turned to Elsie with puffy eyes.

"What if Doris never recovers emotionally from this? What if she's unable to conceive again?"

"We must pray for her and try to think positive. If it's meant for Doris and Brian to have a *boppli,* then it will happen in God's time."

"You're right. Larry and I never expected to be blessed with another child after Scott was born. The doctor said due to the damage done to my uterus, it wasn't likely I'd get pregnant again." Arlene smiled, despite her tears. "Then eight years later, along came baby Samuel."

Elsie nodded as she reached for her sister's hand. "You've been blessed all right."

"Doris is going to need our help

when she leaves the hospital in a few days. That means we'll have to put looking for Dad's will on hold for a while."

"It's not a priority right now." Elsie was sure their brother wouldn't be happy about the delay, but it couldn't be helped. Their sister's needs came first. She would give Joel a call later on and tell him what happened.

Akron, Ohio

Joel had been sneezing and blowing his nose so much it felt raw. He hated being sick — especially while spending Thanksgiving alone with a less-than-exciting frozen dinner. With only the company of his television set during the holiday, he'd given in to self-pity. Kristi was probably at her folks', eating a moist turkey dinner with all the trimmings, while he sat at home on the couch with a box of tissues and a bottle of cough syrup that was six months past its sell-by date. Joel didn't care how old the stuff was; he needed something to relieve his nagging cough.

Pulling himself off the couch, he ambled out to the kitchen to replenish his glass of water. He remembered how his mother used to stress the importance of staying hydrated when a person had a cold or the flu. Joel felt like he had both, because, in addition to coughing and sneezing, his body had begun to ache. "I probably have a fever, too," he mumbled, going to the sink and filling his glass with cold water. He would have taken his temperature, but he'd misplaced the thermometer.

Joel set the glass on the counter and pulled a tissue from his pocket as he felt another sneeze coming on. *Ah-choo! Ah-choo! Ah-choo!* As the final sneeze hit, a muscle in Joel's back spasmed, and he fell to his knees from the pain. *Oh, great! How much worse can it get?*

He gritted his teeth, pulled himself up, and tried to straighten, but the pain was too intense. Walking bent over while holding his back, he shuffled across the room to the refrigerator. He grabbed an ice pack from the freezer compartment and wrapped it in a dishtowel. Since the living room was closer than Joel's bedroom, he headed in that direction, grimacing as he inched his way along. When he reached the couch, he somehow managed to lie down and stuff the ice pack behind his back. This was one time Joel was glad he didn't have any work lined up for a few days. It would give him time to recover from the pain surging up and down his back. But it would be a long weekend, being alone and feeling so miserable.

Joel wished he could lie back on the sofa and relax while someone tended to his every need — making sure he was fed and being there to keep him company. He would have had the help he needed if he hadn't lost the special woman in his life.

Pouting, Joel glanced at his cell phone lying on the coffee table. He thought about calling his friend Tom, but Tom had gone out of town to spend Thanksgiving with his family and wouldn't be back until Sunday evening.

Maybe I should call Kristi. If she knows I'm not feeling well, and that my back's acting up, she might feel sorry for me and come over. It would give me the chance to tell her once again that I'm sorry for messing things up.

Another jolt of pain shot through Joel's back as he reached for the phone. It would be worth the agony if Kristi responded to his call. In desperation, he punched in her number and held his breath. Several rings later, her voice mail picked up. "Kristi, it's Joel," he said, groaning. "I have a bad cold, and during a sneezing attack, my back went out. I'm really miserable and barely able to function. Would you please come over to my place and put your nursing skills to work so I'll feel better?" He paused, searching for the right words. "Please call me or drop by. I really need you, Kristi."

When Joel hung up, he kept the cell phone by his side so he wouldn't have to reach for it if she called.

"Was that your cell phone I heard

buzzing?" Kristi's dad asked as they sat at the dining-room table eating pumpkin pie and drinking hot chocolate.

"It may have been." She scooped a dollop of Mom's homemade whipped cream off her pie and dropped it into her cup. "I turned the ringer off before I put the phone in my purse so I wouldn't be bothered with any calls while I'm here." Truthfully, Kristi half expected Joel to call, and he was the last person she wanted to talk to today. Even though he hadn't called her for several days, she had a hunch, with this being a holiday they'd previously spent together, he might get nostalgic and decide to call.

"Why don't we play a card game after we finish our dessert?" Kristi's mother suggested. "All the food we ate today has made me sleepy, and a rousing game is what I need to keep awake."

Dad yawned and leaned back in his chair. "I'm with you, JoAnn. There's something about eating turkey. Even if I don't stuff myself, it causes me to feel like I need a nap."

"It's the tryptophan," Kristi said. "Tryptophan is an amino acid found in turkey, and it's known for making people sleepy."

"Our daughter's smart." Mom smiled at Kristi. "I'll bet you learned that in nurses' training."

"I may have, but it's something I

read about a long time ago in a magazine article." Kristi stirred her hot chocolate and took a drink. "Yum. I like it when you whip heavy cream. It's much better than the spray kind you buy in a can, and I like the subtle way you sweeten it, without too much sugar or vanilla."

Mom's smile widened. "I enjoy cooking for you and your dad, and I'm glad you appreciate it."

"I appreciate it, too." Dad reached over and helped himself to the fluffy white topping, added some to his mug, and took a drink. "Ah . . . now that's what I call good."

Thinking about all the delicious food she'd just shared with Mom and Dad caused Kristi to reflect on one of the patients at the nursing home where she worked. *I wonder if Audrey felt up to eating any turkey today. Poor thing. She looked so pale when I checked on her yesterday.*

"Is anything wrong?" Mom tapped Kristi's arm. "You look so serious all of a sudden."

Kristi slumped in her chair. "I was thinking about my patient, Audrey, who's dying of cancer. I'm sure I mentioned her before."

"You did. Has she gotten worse?" Mom's gentle tone revealed her concern.

"Yes. Up until recently, she's been able to be out of bed and get around on her own, but now she's pretty much bedridden."

"Cancer's an ugly thing." Dad spoke up. "Seems like there's hardly a family who hasn't been touched by it."

"I know." Kristi sighed. "I've been praying for a miracle on Audrey's behalf, but with her getting worse, I have to think my prayer won't be answered."

"All prayers are answered," Dad reminded. "Just not always the way we would like."

Kristi thought about Joel again and how she'd been praying for him, as Audrey suggested. It had only been a little over a month since they'd broken up, so he was still fresh on her mind. She continued to wonder if anything in his life had changed. Obviously, Joel wouldn't be a different person right away, but maybe he'd receive the help he needed from God sometime soon. Before Joel could change, however, he had to let Jesus come into his heart.

Redirecting her thoughts, she smiled and said, "As much as I'll miss Audrey when she's gone, I'm convinced she's a Christian and will be in a better place. She's told me more than once that she's ready to go home and be with the Lord."

"The sting of death lessens a bit when we know someone we care about has been transported to heaven." Dad reached for the pot of hot chocolate in the middle of the table and poured himself another cup.

Kristi finished eating her pie and pushed away from the table. "I'll take my dishes to the sink and then get out one of our favorite games." Hopefully once they started playing, she could concentrate on something more uplifting.

After she rinsed her dishes, Kristi decided to check her phone messages, in case someone from the nursing home had called with an update on Audrey's condition. Dorine was working this evening and had promised to let Kristi know if Audrey took a turn for the worst.

Listening to the only message she'd received, Kristi inhaled a long breath when she heard Joel's voice.

She took a seat at the kitchen table and pressed the phone closer to her ear. For a split second, hearing him say he wasn't feeling well touched a soft spot in her heart and she felt pity for him. Kristi was aware of how miserable a person felt when they had a bad cold, much less a sore back. But common sense kicked in when she remembered Joel lying to her about why he'd taken money from their joint account. He was probably either making up the situation, or using it as a means to get her there so he could try and talk her into taking him back.

Kristi's lips pressed together as she pushed her shoulders against the back of the chair. *Sorry, Joel, but it's not going to work. I'm staying right here for the rest of the evening.*

CHAPTER 2

Berlin, Ohio

"How are you feeling? Are you comfortable there on the couch, or would you rather lie on your bed?"

Doris clenched her teeth in an effort to keep from shouting. Today was Monday, the last day of November, and she'd only been home from the hospital a few hours. But in those few hours, all her sister Elsie had done was fuss. *How does she think I feel? I'm laid up with a broken leg and sore head. Worse than that, my hopes of giving Brian a baby have been destroyed.* "I'm fine here on the couch for now," she murmured.

Elsie placed a pillow under her cast, with a reminder that the doctor said she should keep her leg elevated as much as possible. "You'll probably have less pain that way, and it will help with the swelling."

"*Jah,* okay." Doris blinked back tears threatening to spill over. *It won't help the pain in my heart, though, will it?*

"Is there anything you need me to bring you before I wash the breakfast dishes?"

"No, I don't need a thing." *Except my baby.* Since Doris had been pregnant less than twenty-four weeks, there would be no funeral. In some ways, she saw it as a blessing, for she wouldn't have to endure the agony of watching a tiny coffin being lowered into the ground. On the other hand, a funeral service brought closure.

Elsie placed her hand gently on Doris's shoulder. "Arlene should be here soon, and then the two of us can do your laundry and get some cleaning done."

After her sister got busy in the kitchen, Doris sat on the sofa awhile, pondering the loss of her unborn child. With the aid of her crutches, she pulled herself up and made her way down the hall to the room next to her and Brian's. It would have been the baby's nursery.

Inside the doorway, Doris paused and looked around the small room with anguish. Her vision blurred as she gazed at the wall where the crib would have gone. Across from it, Brian had placed a rocking chair — the same one he had been rocked in as a baby. Doris's leg throbbed as she hobbled over to the chair and collapsed into it. Strong sobs shook her body. Her heart felt as if it was broken in two. She thought her tears would never stop flowing. So many feelings hit her all at once; it was hard to feel any hope.

In no time it seemed, both of Doris's sisters were at her side.

Arlene, wearing her jacket and outer bonnet, held baby Samuel in her arms and placed him gently on Doris's lap. "Will you hold him for me awhile?"

Doris sniffed. "Jah, of course."

Elsie and Arlene stood quietly beside her, looking down as she rocked the baby. Doris found comfort in the little guy's chubby, warm body. Did Arlene know how fortunate she was?

"What about the sorting we'd all planned to do at Dad's house this week?" she asked, looking up at Elsie. "How's that going to get done if you two are here helping me?"

"It can wait. Right now, your needs take priority over finding

Dad's will."

"I bet Joel won't be happy about that."

"I still haven't called him, but I need to do it soon."

Doris figured Elsie had put off making the call because she dreaded Joel's reaction to the news that the search for the will had been suspended. She couldn't blame her. Their brother could be quite difficult when he didn't get his way.

"I'm worried about Doris," Arlene said after she and Elsie had gotten their sister settled on the living-room couch and gone to the kitchen.

"She looked tired, so hopefully

she'll sleep awhile," Elsie replied.

Arlene had brought the baby to the kitchen with them so Doris could rest. "I hope Samuel doesn't get fussy and wake her. With my older children in school and Larry at work, I didn't have anyone to watch him today."

"I'm sure it'll be fine. We can set his playpen up here in the kitchen, if you brought it."

"Jah, it's in my buggy. I'll go get it." Arlene handed Samuel to Elsie and went out the door.

Elsie looked at the precious infant in her arms. The little guy's eyes closed slowly then opened. He was no doubt ready for a nap. "You're so adorable and sweet," she whispered, reflecting on how soothing it felt when her children were babies.

A short time later, Arlene returned with the playpen. Elsie waited for her to set it up before passing the little one to his mother.

"When I finish the dishes, we can move him to whatever room we decide to clean."

"That's a good idea." Arlene placed the baby in the playpen, then grabbed a dishtowel to dry the dishes. "I feel sorry for Doris. She wanted a boppli so badly."

Elsie's chest felt heavy. She stared at the sponge she held. "It's hard to stay positive during times like these, but for our sister's sake, we must encourage her to look for the good in things. As Dad used to say,

'This too will pass, and things are bound to go better soon.' "

Akron

Joel blinked against the light streaming through the blinds in his living-room. He'd spent another miserable night on the couch, which had probably done his back more harm than good.

Groaning, he forced himself to sit up and winced when he tried to straighten. *How am I going to do any work today when I'm still in pain?* Joel had spent the last four days alternating between using a heating pad and an ice pack on his back. *Probably should see a chiropractor, massage therapist, or doctor — maybe all three. This isn't getting better on its own.*

Joel rubbed the sides and top of his head. His hair felt greasy. He really ought to take a shower, but his back hurt worse when he stood too long. His cold lingered, which didn't help, either. He wished he could call on someone to take care of him. He'd tried calling Kristi several times over the weekend, but she hadn't returned even one of his calls. He'd called Tom last night, but his friend couldn't help because he'd gotten stuck at his folks' in bad weather and didn't know when he'd make it home.

Guess I could call one of my sisters, but they'd have to hire a driver to bring them here. He winced. *Bet they wouldn't even care that I'm here alone with a bad back and a horrible cold.*

Joel picked up his cell phone and searched for local chiropractors. He found one a few miles from where he lived and dialed the number. After explaining his predicament, he was given an appointment for three o'clock that afternoon. It would not be easy, but somehow he'd muster the strength to drive there. In the meantime, he would force himself to take a shower and put on some clean clothes. He wrinkled his nose. "Bet I smell as bad as I look."

"How'd your weekend go? Did you have a nice Thanksgiving?" Dorine asked when Kristi arrived at the nursing home.

"It was good. I spent Thanksgiving Day with my parents, went shopping on Friday, attended another quilting class with my mom Saturday, and had dinner at my folks' house after church on Sunday." Kristi smiled. "How was yours?"

Dorine pressed her palm against her chest. "Thanksgiving was kind of rough here at work, and when I had a late meal at my boyfriend's house that evening, I had a hard time feeling thankful."

"What happened?"

"Mr. Riggins had a heart attack and was rushed to the hospital." Pausing to pick up a magazine someone had dropped on the floor,

Dorine's shoulders drooped. "It happened in the lunchroom, and the patients who were eating there became quite upset. It took a while to get them settled down."

"I'm sorry to hear it." Kristi spoke softly. "Have you heard how he's doing?"

"No, but then I was off Friday, Saturday, and Sunday, same as you."

"What about Audrey? How's she doing?" Kristi slipped off her hat and matching gloves, as well as her coat, and put them away.

Dorine gave a slow shake of her head. "She was in a lot of pain on Thanksgiving, and the medication kept her sleeping most of the day. She's getting nourishment from her

IV, but even when she's awake, she doesn't want to eat anything."

Kristi's arms pressed tightly against her sides. "I wish I had worked Thanksgiving. I could have sat with her awhile and maybe coaxed her to eat a little something."

"It wouldn't have done any good, Kristi. Short of a miracle, Audrey doesn't have much longer to live." Dorine's eyes filled with sadness as she looked down the hall toward Audrey's room.

Tears stung Kristi's eyes, but she tried to suppress her emotions. She enjoyed tending to the patients who lived here, but at times such as this, she felt like quitting her job and looking for work that didn't involve sickness and death. It was hard not to become depressed while performing her nursing duties — especially when faced with the imminent death of Audrey, who had helped her get through the breakup with Joel. "Think I'll go to Audrey's room right now to check on her."

"Go right ahead, but don't be surprised if you find her sleeping."

As Kristi started down the hall, Dorine called, "Hey, Kristi, before you go, I could use a little help." She pushed the vitals cart along.

Kristi paused. "Sure, what do you need?"

"A new patient came in earlier, and I could use your help turning him. He was transferred here from the hospital and needs a lot of assistance right now."

"Okay, I'll follow you in." Kristi motioned for Dorine to lead the way.

When they finished getting the gentleman situated a short time later, Kristi headed down the hall to see Audrey. She found the dear woman in bed, hooked up to an IV. Her eyes were shut. Her skin was nearly as pale as the bed sheets.

Kristi stood at the foot of Audrey's bed and closed her eyes. *Heavenly Father, as much as I want to keep her here, please don't let Audrey suffer. If it's not Your will to heal her, then please take her home to be with You.*

She kept her eyes closed and reflected on the times Audrey had ministered to her when she'd been trying to deal with the end of her relationship with Joel. "If only there was something I could do for you," she whispered.

"There is. You can sit beside my bed."

Kristi's eyes snapped open. She was surprised to see the elderly woman looking at her, a slight smile on her thin lips. "Oh, you're awake. I'm sorry if I disturbed you."

Audrey lifted a bony finger, beckoning her to come closer.

Kristi took a seat beside the bed and reached out to clasp this special patient's hand.

"Where have you been? It seems like such a long time ago that we talked." Audrey spoke so faintly, Kristi had to lean closer in order to make out her words.

"I spent Thanksgiving with my parents, and then I had Friday, Saturday, and Sunday off. I'll be working for the next five days, so we'll get to see each other often."

"The cancer's getting worse. My time is drawing close." Audrey's breathing was raspy. Kristi could tell it was all she could do to keep her eyes open.

"You don't need to talk. I'll just sit here with you and hold your hand." Kristi struggled to keep from breaking down. It was difficult to see how quickly this sweet lady had gone downhill.

"I — I wish I could be up and

around. I don't like being stuck in this bed. It makes me feel worthless."

Kristi gently patted Audrey's cold hand. "You are not worthless. Your comforting words and heartfelt prayers have been a big help to me." She glanced away briefly, blinking to keep tears from falling onto her cheeks. This was not a time to give in to her emotions. She wanted to be strong for Audrey's sake.

"Are you still praying for that young man — Joel, isn't that his name?"

"Yes, I've been praying." Kristi chose not to mention that Joel had called several times over the weekend and left messages. He'd sounded so desperate, it had been hard not to return his calls. But Kristi felt sure he'd only been trying to prey on her sympathy in hopes of getting her back. In one of his messages, Joel had said he'd changed and would never say or do anything to hurt her again. Words were cheap. Joel had done nothing to prove he'd changed. Even if he had, Kristi wasn't sure she could ever believe him. *A zebra doesn't change its stripes.* She brought her hand up to her chest. *If he really had changed, he wouldn't have quit coming to church.*

Turning her focus back to Audrey, Kristi said, "I've been praying for you, too."

"Thank you, dear." Audrey's eyelids fluttered, then closed.

Kristi could tell she had fallen asleep by the way her chest rose slowly and fell. Thinking the gentle woman needed her rest, she stood and slipped quietly out of the room. She would check on Audrey a little later. Right now, other patients needed her care.

CHAPTER 3

Millersburg, Ohio

Elsie shivered, covering herself with her shawl as she hurried down the driveway to the phone shack. It had been a week since Doris got out of the hospital, and she still needed help. But Elsie noticed some improvement. Doris got around better on her crutches. Her color was back, too, and she appeared to be more rested. Of course, her broken leg and bumped head would mend, but it would take longer for Doris's heart to heal after the loss of her baby. She and Brian would continue to need their family for spiritual and moral support in the days ahead.

As soon as Elsie checked for messages, she'd head for Doris's house. Arlene would join her again, only this time instead of cleaning, they planned on baking. Christmas was less than three weeks away, so baking some things ahead and freezing them would jumpstart their holiday preparations.

She stepped into the phone shack, glancing quickly around for spiders lurking about, and turned on the answering machine. There was only one message — from Joel. Elsie suspected he'd called to ask if the will had been found. She brought her hand up to her cheek. *I should have called him before now.* Every time she'd thought to do it, something came up and it didn't get done.

As Elsie listened to the message, her jaw clenched. *Is that all he ever thinks about?* With a feeling of dread, she dialed Joel's number. Elsie was surprised when he picked up the phone. Quite often when she called, she would get his voice mail.

"Hi, Joel, it's Elsie."

"Oh, good. I'm glad you called. I've been lying around with a bad back and a cold, wondering if you've found the will." His voice sounded raspy, like he'd been coughing a lot.

"Are you okay?"

"I'm some better, but I was pretty much flat on my back for the better part of a week."

"I'm sorry to hear that."

"So, about Dad's will . . . Have you had any luck?"

Elsie shook her head over Joel's misplaced priorities. "Doris fell down the stairs on Thanksgiving, so the search for the will has been postponed until she's fully recovered."

Silence on the other end.

"Joel, did you hear what I said?"

"Yeah. Is Doris hurt bad?"

"She broke her leg. Worse than that, she lost her boppli."

"What baby?"

Elsie wrapped her finger around the phone cord and swallowed hard. It was difficult to talk about it — especially with Joel, whom she was sure wouldn't understand.

"I didn't know she was expecting a baby."

"Doris found out she was expecting a few weeks ago. Since she and Brian have been married over six years, they didn't think they could have any children." Her shoulders slumped as she continued to speak. "They were so excited about it, and now their hopes have been crushed."

"I'm sorry to hear this, but I'm also disappointed I wasn't notified of her pregnancy or told that she'd fallen and lost the baby." He coughed a couple of times and let out a heavy sigh.

Elsie heard the frustration in her brother's voice. "I'm sorry, Joel. I assumed Doris had told you when she found out she was pregnant." She paused for a breath. "It's no excuse, but things have been hectic since her accident. Arlene and I have been going over to help Doris every day, so I kept forgetting to call you."

Once more, the phone became silent on the other end.

"Joel, are you still there?"

"Yeah. Just trying to process all this. I'll try to stop by and see Doris as soon as I have some free time. Thanks to my back going out, I lost a week's worth of work, so there's some catching up to do. I need money coming in more than anything right now."

She gripped the phone so tightly her fingers throbbed. Hearing him reminded her of the funeral — the way Joel had disregarded their father's passing for the sake of getting his share of the inheritance. Even when he made an effort to be sympathetic, his own needs always came first. *If your family was important to you, you'd make the time to see Doris right away,* she thought with regret.

Joel cleared his throat. "About the missing will . . . Since you and Arlene are busy helping Doris right now, maybe I should go over to Dad's place and search for it again."

Elsie's jaw clenched. "So you don't have time to see Doris right now, but you could make time to search for the will?"

"Well, I —"

"How can you even be thinking about Dad's will when our sister is in pain and grieving the loss of her baby?" Elsie was ready to slam the receiver and end this conversation. She'd had enough of Joel being so self-centered, especially toward their family. But she drew in a slow, steady breath and allowed her brother to respond.

"Okay, you're right, but before we hang up, I was wondering what you would think about selling Dad's horses."

"What?" Her voice grew sharper. "Why are you bringing that up?" *What is he thinking?*

"Because we could all use the money — especially Doris. I'm sure she's gonna have some hospital and doctor bills to pay." Joel's tone grew louder, too.

Elsie sighed in frustration. "Until Dad's will is found and we know how he wanted things divided up, we should not sell anything. I'm sure our sisters would agree with me on that."

He grunted. "Of course they would. You three have always sided against me."

She couldn't argue the point, but it was because Joel had made so many unwise decisions and given unreasonable demands. It would be easier for Elsie to side with him if he put others' needs ahead of his own.

"Listen, I need to bid on a job right now. I'll forget about Dad's will for the moment. Let me know when you're ready to start looking for it again." Joel hung up without saying goodbye.

Elsie pressed down on the receiver and got up from her chair. Her muscles were tight, and her toes felt numb when she stepped out of the phone shack. The conversation with Joel had been unnerving, but she didn't have time to dwell on it. Elsie wished she could count on her brother to go and see Doris. If she told her sister Joel might drop by for a visit, Doris would be disappointed if he didn't follow through. Elsie was hesitant to say anything, so she decided to remain silent on the subject. Right now, she needed to go to Doris's house and see how she was doing.

Berlin

"Here's a cozy coverlet you can rest under while we're waiting for your husband to get here. Is there anything else I can do for you before I head home?" Arlene asked as she gathered up her things.

"No, you and Elsie did enough today with all the baking you got done." Doris placed the small covering next to her on the recliner. "Brian will be here soon, so you should both go home and tend to your families." Doris had spent part of the day in the kitchen, with her broken leg propped on a stool, so she could visit with her sisters. The rest of the time she'd rested in Brian's recliner. Sitting around so much got on her nerves. Doris had always been a doer, and watching others do all the work she should have been doing herself made her feel even worse.

Another thing that really bothered Doris was seeing Arlene's baby, Samuel, laughing and rolling about in his playpen. It was wrong to be jealous, but she couldn't help herself. She wanted nothing more than to have a child of her own and struggled with the thought that it might never happen.

Elsie stepped in front of Doris's chair. "Are you sure you don't want one of us to stay until Brian gets home from work? I'd be happy to do that."

"No, you go ahead. I'll stay right here in the recliner until he arrives, so don't worry about me."

Both sisters hesitated but finally nodded. "We'll be back tomorrow, so don't try to do anything on your own," Arlene said.

She held up one hand. "I promise."

After Elsie and Arlene left, Doris leaned her head back and closed her eyes, feeling drowsy. She was almost to the point of dozing off, when a knock sounded on the door, jolting her upright. Needing to see who it was, she grabbed her crutches and stood. When she hobbled across the room and opened the door, she was surprised to see her friend Anna on the porch.

"I've wanted to come by and see how you're doing," Anna said breathlessly, "but things have been busy at the schoolhouse with the Christmas program coming up soon, and I couldn't get away."

"Well, you're here now, and I'm glad to see you." Doris gestured with her head toward the living room. "Come inside and we can sit and visit."

"Jah, we do need to sit, because you should get off your feet." Anna removed her outer garments and draped them over a chair. "How are you feeling? Is your leg still painful?"

"It hurts sometimes," Doris admitted. "It feels better when I keep it propped up." She took a seat in the recliner, and Anna seated herself on the couch across from her.

"How are things at school? Do all the scholars know their parts for the program?"

"Some do, but others are having a hard time remembering their recitations." Anna smiled. "I'm sure everyone will do fine on the evening of the program, though."

"I remember when I was nine years old I was given a poem to recite. When I looked out and saw my parents that evening, I became *naerfich* and forgot what I was supposed to say." Doris rubbed the bridge of her nose, as the embarrassment of the moment came back to her. She'd taken some teasing from Joel on the way home, and of course, he'd bragged about the fact that he'd done well with his part.

"I felt nervous during some of my Christmas programs when I was a girl, too." Anna sat quietly, as though pondering something. Then she looked at Doris and said, "I'm sorry you lost your boppli. I know how much you looked forward to becoming a *mamm*."

Tears welled in Doris's eyes, but she tilted her head up and blinked to prevent them from falling onto her cheeks. "It's hard to say this, but I guess it was not meant to be. Maybe Brian and I aren't supposed to have any *kinner.*"

"Is that what you really think, or is it your way of accepting what happened?"

"I–I'm not sure. My desire to be a parent hasn't left, but I need to accept whatever God's will is for me and Brian."

Anna nodded slowly, as a flush of crimson color crept across her cheeks. "I understand. I've had to work through my feelings for Joel and accept the fact that he and I are not meant to be together. He's engaged to marry someone else now, so there's no hope of us ever being together."

"Actually, he's not engaged any-more." Feeling a sudden chill, Doris picked up the coverlet and placed it over her knees, appreciating the warmth it offered.

"Really?" Anna's eyes widened. "What happened?"

"It's not my place to give the details, but I don't think Joel and Kristi will be getting back together."

"Can you tell me this much — did he break up with her, the same way as he did me?"

"No, it was Kristi who ended their relationship."

Anna glanced out the window, then looked directly at Doris. "Do you think . . . ? Is there any chance Joel might return to the

Amish faith?"

"I honestly doubt it." Doris wanted to say there was a possibility Joel might return and show an interest in Anna again, but he had given no signs of making such a change. Even if he had, she couldn't imagine him giving up his modern ways for the plain life — not after he'd been gone for more than seven years.

"I need to forget about Joel and move on with my life, don't I?" Anna's chin quivered.

"Jah, I believe you should. It's the right thing to do."

Akron

As Joel left the jobsite and headed for the bank, he felt thankful he was finally able to work again; although he still had to take it easy. The last thing he wanted to do was reinjure his back and end up out of commission once more. He'd been paid for the first half of a kitchen remodel and wanted to put the money in the bank.

I'll put it in our joint account, he decided. *If Kristi checks on the balance again, and discovers I've put some of the money back that I previously took out, maybe she'll decide I'm deserving of a second chance.*

A short time later, Joel pulled into a space in the bank's parking lot and walked into the building. When he reached the first available teller, he explained, "I'd like to deposit a check into the joint account I have with Kristi Palmer."

When the middle-aged woman gave him a blank stare, he realized she needed the account number. Having memorized it from previous deposits he had made, Joel gave her the information.

Peering at him through her metal-framed glasses, she let out a soft breath and turned to the computer, entering the necessary data. She looked back at Joel and squinted. "I'm sorry, sir, but that account's been closed."

"What?" His arm jerked, and he felt sweat bead on his forehead. "Are — are you sure?"

She gave a brief nod. "According to the statement on the computer, Miss Palmer closed the account several days ago."

That's just great. Joel rubbed the side of his neck. *Is she trying to send me a message?*

"Is there anything else I can do for you, Mr. Byler?"

"What?" Joel jerked his head.

She repeated herself.

"Uh, sure. I'll put this check in my business account." He gave her the number and rolled his shoulders in an attempt to shake away some of the tension he felt. *Maybe it's really over between me and Kristi. Is it time to move on with my life?*

CHAPTER 4

The second Sunday of December found Kristi at her parents' home, sharing a meal after church. Ever since she and Joel had broken up, Sunday dinners had become a regular occurrence. Last year during the holidays, Kristi and Joel had driven around, looking at Christmas lights. They'd picked out two trees — one to put in her condo and one for Joel's single-wide. She remembered how they'd stayed up late to ring in the New Year, making a toast with sparkling cider at midnight. Those times together had been fun, but Kristi needed to start fresh, without Joel in the picture.

She felt thankful her parents were Christians and had always been there when she had a need. Although the pain of losing Joel had lessened, at times she missed what they'd once had.

"You're not eating much today. Is the roast not tender enough?"

Mom's question scattered Kristi's thoughts, and she nearly lost her grip on the fork she held. "Uh, no, it's fine." She took a bite of meat and blotted her lips with her napkin. "Really good, in fact."

"Did you get a chance to greet our new youth pastor when church let out?" Mom asked. "His name is Darin Underwood, in case you didn't hear it when Pastor Anderson introduced him to the congregation."

"No, I didn't get to meet him today. Too many other people were talking to him, and it would have been awkward if I'd barged in." Kristi brought her glass to her lips and sipped some water.

"I spoke with Darin for a few minutes before church started." Dad picked up the salt shaker and sprinkled some on his meat. Then he glanced briefly at Mom, as though expecting her to say something. Dad's blood pressure had been running a little on the high side lately, and the doctor suggested he cut down on salt and get more exercise. He'd joined the fitness center where Kristi sometimes went, but giving up salt seemed to be hard for him.

Mom didn't say anything, but her narrowed eyes spoke volumes.

They ate in silence for a while, with only the sounds of utensils clinking against their plates. Then Mom looked at Kristi and said, "I've been thinking about inviting the new youth pastor over for a meal soon. It will give us a chance to get to know him better. I hope you'll be free to join us that evening." She nudged Kristi's arm. "Darin is single, you know."

"I hope you're not trying to play matchmaker, Mom." Kristi

groaned. "As I've mentioned before, I'm not ready to pursue a relationship right now."

Mom's cheeks colored as she picked up her glass. "I'm not suggesting anything like that. I only thought —"

"Changing the subject," Kristi interrupted, "have you done much on your own with the quilted pillow slip you're making?"

"A little, but I'll work on it more when we go back to the quilting class this Saturday. Our Amish teacher is so patient and good at what she does." Mom chuckled. "I'll bet she could sew a quilt in her sleep."

Kristi smiled. "The quilt I'm making for my bed will take longer to make than our six-week class allows, so I've been working on it at home in the evenings."

Dad smiled. "I'm glad my two favorite ladies have found something they can enjoy doing together."

"It's been fun, and after each lesson Mom and I try out a different restaurant in Amish country." Kristi fiddled with her dress sleeve. They hadn't been back to Der Dutchman in Walnut Creek since they'd seen Doris, but she hoped they could go there again sometime.

Berlin

"I'm glad you were able to make it to church today, but you must be tired." Arlene followed her sister to the couch. Once Doris was stretched out, she put a pillow under her leg.

Doris nodded. "The trip there was tiring, and sitting for three hours wore me out. That's why Brian and I didn't stay for the meal."

"Is there something I can fix for you now?"

"No, Brian heated some soup for us as soon as we got home. What about you? Did you have a chance to eat with your family before you came over here?" Doris asked.

"Jah. When I saw you leave, we decided not to stay for the meal, either." Arlene leaned back in the rocking chair and started it moving slowly. "After we got home, I fixed sandwiches for everyone, fed and diapered Samuel, and then put him down for a nap. If he wakes up before I get back, Larry or one of the girls will keep him occupied until I get back."

Doris yawned and covered her mouth with her hand. "You really didn't have to come here today. Brian's with me. If I need anything, he'll take care of it."

"I know, but I wasn't sure if you'd eaten, so —"

"A van just pulled into the yard," Brian announced as he walked into the room. "It's your aunt," he said, looking out the living-room window. "She's getting out of the vehicle."

Arlene hopped up. "I wonder

what she's doing here." She turned to Doris. "Did you know Aunt Verna was coming?"

Doris shook her head.

"Guess we'll find out the reason for her visit soon enough." Brian opened the door and stepped outside.

Arlene grabbed her shawl and followed. Aunt Verna was walking toward the house with her suitcase, which Brian was quick to take from her.

"Are you surprised to see me?" Aunt Verna gave Arlene a hug.

"I certainly am. Neither Doris nor I knew you were coming. Does Elsie know?"

"Nope. When I heard about Doris's accident, I decided she could probably use some help, so I talked it over with Lester, and he said I could come for as long as I'm needed." She grinned. "I talked to him about joining me here for Christmas, and he agreed. He will be here on Christmas Eve. It'll be nice to spend the holiday with our three special nieces."

Arlene gently squeezed her aunt's hand. "Having you both here will be *wunderbaar,* and your help will certainly be appreciated."

As Joel drove through the town of Berlin, memories of the past flooded his mind. As a teenager, he and some of his buddies came here for pizza and to hang out together. *Those days were carefree,* he thought, turning onto the road that led to Doris's house. While he'd never had enough money to satisfy his wants, Joel had been better off than he was right now. At least back then he wasn't faced with a bunch of debts he couldn't pay. Life seemed much simpler when he was still Amish.

Joel slowed to turn onto Doris and Brian's driveway. Their place was small compared to most of the Amish homes he'd been in, but they didn't need much space since only the two of them lived there. *Too bad she lost her baby,* he thought. *I bet Brian would have happily added onto the house if they needed more room for a growing family.*

He pulled up next to the barn and turned off the ignition. Joel had driven his everyday car today, knowing better than to show his fancy Corvette to any of his family. He hoped his visit with Doris would go well and that he'd have the right words to say. Joel had never been good at communicating with Doris — at least not since they'd become adults. He always sensed her resentment of him for having left the Amish faith. It didn't help that his former girlfriend, Anna Detweiler, was Doris's best friend. *Doris probably hasn't forgiven me for turning my back on Anna and our relationship.*

Determined to make the best of this visit, Joel grabbed the "Get

Well" balloon he'd bought and got out of the car. He knocked on the door and was startled when he was greeted by Aunt Verna.

"I'm surprised to see you here," they said in unison.

Joel's cheeks heated. Apparently his aunt was aware that he didn't come around very often. "I came to see how Doris is doing."

She tipped her head to one side. "What was that?"

"I said, 'I came to see how Doris is doing.' " Joel spoke a little louder this time. "Just didn't expect you to be here."

She smiled and gave him a hug. "I got here a short time ago. Came to help out so your sisters could have a break. With Christmas coming soon, they'll have lots to do at their own homes, so I'll take care of things here."

"I'm sure your help will be appreciated." Joel patted her back, continuing to speak loud enough for her to hear. "It's good to see you."

"Come inside and say hello to Doris. You just missed Arlene. She went home a few minutes ago." Aunt Verna led the way to the living room, where Joel found his sister on the couch, with Brian sitting on the end of it by her feet.

Joel moved over to stand beside Doris and handed her the balloon. "This is for you. I heard about your accident and wanted to come by and see how you're doing."

"Thank you. I'm getting along as well as can be expected." Clinging to the balloon, she clasped her hands tightly together in her lap.

"I'm sorry for your loss."

Doris gave a brief nod in response.

"Please, take a seat." Brian gestured to the recliner near the rocker, where Aunt Verna sat.

Scraping a hand through his hair, Joel did as his brother-in-law suggested. He'd been right to visit, but he felt strangely out of place. Sometimes when he was around his siblings and their spouses, things became heated. Other times, his tension and sense of being out of place dissipated.

"How have you been, Joel?" Aunt

Verna asked.

"I'm gettin' by." *But things would be better if I had more money.*

"Did you say you're going to buy something?"

"No, I said I'm getting by."

She smiled at him. "Glad to hear it. How's that pretty young woman who was with you at my *bruder's* funeral? Kristi — isn't that her name?"

Joel winced at the mention of Kristi. "We broke up," he mumbled, hoping to keep his composure.

"What was that?" Aunt Verna cupped one hand around her ear.

"He said they broke up." Doris turned to Joel and frowned. "You seem to have a knack for messing

85

things up with the people you're supposed to love."

As soon as the words were out of her mouth, a sharp pain hit Joel in the chest. His sister was right. There was no denying it. This whole time he'd been attempting to get Kristi back because he was lonely without her. He'd ruined the chance of marrying the woman he loved, all for the sake of having money. It was likely he would never hold Kristi in his arms again, and that pained him the most.

Doris gasped. "I–I'm sorry, Joel. I shouldn't have said that."

Shrugging, he stared at his shoes. "You only spoke what you feel is true. I don't have a good track record with women. Apparently you felt the need to remind me of that."

"Maybe we need to change the subject," Brian interjected.

"Or maybe it would be best if I go." Joel stood and looked at Doris. "I hope your leg heals as it should and that you'll feel better soon." He said a quick goodbye and hurried out the door.

"Probably shouldn't have come here," he muttered, while opening his car door. *I'm glad Doris is doing okay, but I'm tired of her putting me down for my mistakes. I never seem to say or do the right thing when I'm around any of my family. Don't know why I bother to try. Even after all this time, Doris is obviously still upset with me for breaking up with Anna.*

As Joel drove down the driveway, he met an Amish buggy heading toward him. He moved the car over as far as he could to let it pass. As the buggy went by, he recognized the driver. It was Anna. *What are the odds?* Joel's toes curled inside his shoes. Not knowing what else to do, he gave a wave and continued out onto the road.

As he traveled on, Joel thought about Anna and all the Sunday afternoons they'd spent together when they were courting. A lot of history lay between them, and every time he saw her, scenes from the past would rush through his head. They'd had some fun times back then, even after Joel became dissatisfied with his life. Before he left the Amish faith, he thought he could convince Anna to go English, too. They could have started a new life together. Anna's experience with children might have helped her get a job as a nanny or working at a daycare center. But Joel now recognized that she would never have agreed to leave. She was committed to the old ways.

He gripped the steering wheel and gritted his teeth. *I shouldn't be thinking about this right now. I'm not Amish anymore, and it's over between me and Anna. There's no going back.*

CHAPTER 5

Charm, Ohio

The following day, when Elsie arrived at Dad's house to do more sorting, she was surprised to see Arlene's buggy parked by the barn. It was the first time since Doris's accident that they'd been able to continue searching for the will. Thanks to Aunt Verna showing up and offering to care for Doris, Elsie and Arlene felt free to spend time here again. They could only be at Dad's a few days a week, however.

With Christmas drawing closer, there was much to be done at home in preparation for the big day.

After Elsie put her horse away in the corral, she grabbed the basket of food she'd brought and went into the house. Arlene sat in the living room, going through a stack of magazines.

"Sorry I'm a little late." Elsie set the basket down, removed her jacket and bonnet, and hung them on a wall peg near the door. "I hope you haven't been working on your own for long."

"No — only fifteen minutes or so." Arlene held up one of the magazines. "Just when I think we've come to the end of catalogs and magazines, I find there are more."

"I don't suppose you've found Dad's will in any of them?"

"No will, but I did find this inside the first magazine I went through." Arlene pointed to the dollar bill lying on the coffee table in front of her.

Elsie pursed her lips. "I wonder why Dad would put money inside a magazine."

"Maybe he was preoccupied and didn't realize he'd done it."

"Or perhaps he put it there for safekeeping. I need to put some food in the refrigerator that I brought for Glen, and then we should keep looking." Elsie picked up the basket and headed for the kitchen. After she'd put the food away, she returned to the living room.

"When we decide to take a break, I'll need to change Glen's sheets and make up his bed. He's been busy with work, not to mention taking care of Dad's horses and doing chores around this place, so I want to help out."

Arlene nodded. "That's understandable. I'd do the same if one of my kinner were staying here."

Elsie walked by the front window and looked out. "It will be nice having Aunt Verna and Uncle Lester for Christmas."

"Jah. I enjoy having all the family gathered together for the special holiday, celebrating Jesus' birth."

"Well, I guess we'd better get busy." Elsie grabbed a stack of magazines and took a seat beside her sister. Instead of turning each of the pages, she held the magazine by the bound edge and shook it. To her surprise, several bills fell out. "Wow! We may be on to something here."

She grabbed another magazine and gave it a good shake. Arlene did the same with the one she held. More money came out — mostly dollar bills, but a couple of fives were also included. As they continued going through the magazines, they discovered more, and then the money stopped.

"Guess maybe Dad only put money in those few magazines." Arlene picked up the bills and counted them out loud. "I can't believe it. Two hundred dollars. What should we do with it?"

Elsie shrugged. "I'm not sure. It would probably be best to set it aside for now. You never know. We might find more in the days ahead."

A knock sounded on the door, and Elsie went to answer it. She was surprised to see Ben Yoder, a local taxidermist, holding a pheasant of all things. It took her a few minutes to recognize it, but then she realized it was the same bird she'd found in her dad's freezer several months ago.

"Your *daed* asked me to taxidermy this for him a few months back." Ben held up the pheasant. "Business has been slow lately, so I got it done sooner than expected."

He dipped his head slightly. "Unfortunately, not soon enough for Eustace to enjoy."

Elsie nodded. She would give nearly anything to have her dad back.

"Do you want the pheasant, or should I try to sell it to someone in the area?"

"One of the men or boys in our family might like it. What is the cost?"

"Normally, a bird like this can go for upwards to four hundred dollars, but since it's standing and not in a flying position, I didn't have to do quite as much work." Ben pulled a piece of paper out of his pocket. "This is how much I was planning to charge your daed."

Elsie stared at the paper and blinked. The bill was for two hundred dollars — exactly the amount she and Arlene had found in the magazines this morning. It seemed as if it were meant to be. "If you'll wait right here, I'll get the money."

He gave a nod and handed her the pheasant.

"I need the money we found in Dad's magazines to pay for this," Elsie announced when she returned to the living room. She placed the bird on the coffee table. "Ben Yoder did this up for Dad, and the bill is two hundred dollars — which is exactly how much money we have."

"The last thing we need is a pheasant." Arlene crossed her arms.

"It's a nice reminder of Dad, and maybe one of the men or boys in our family would like it."

Arlene sighed. "Since Ben did the work, I guess we should use the money we found to pay him." She handed Elsie the bills and glanced briefly at the bird. "It sure looks real, doesn't it?"

"Jah. Ben did a good job." Elsie moved toward the door, clutching the money in her hand. "I'd best not keep him waiting on the porch. As soon as I pay him, we can have lunch."

"What should we do next?" Arlene asked when she finished drying their lunch dishes. "We've gone through most of the magazines on the first floor and taken a break. Well, I did anyway, while you took care of Glen's sheets."

Elsie wrung out the sponge and began wiping down the counter closest to the stove. "Guess we could do some more sorting upstairs."

"There're still things in the basement that haven't been gone through."

Elsie shivered. "I'm hoping we can talk the men into cleaning down there because *schpinne* are bound to be lurking about."

Arlene waved the dishtowel at Elsie. "You and your fear of spiders."

"I can't help it. They creep me out."

Rolling her eyes, Arlene reached for the last dish she'd dried and placed it in the cupboard. "Maybe we should take the magazines and catalogs we've already looked through out to the burn barrel. There's no point in keeping them."

"True." Elsie put the sponge away. "Let's put our jackets on and take care of those now. It's a chilly day, and it might feel good to stand around the barrel while the magazines burn."

Arlene chuckled. "Next thing you'll be suggesting we look for some marshmallows to roast."

"You know, that's not a bad idea." Elsie poked her sister's arm. "Just kidding."

After putting on their jackets, they

stacked magazines in a cardboard box and carried it outside.

Arlene was about to light the fire when Henry Raber's tractor pulled in. He climbed down and headed their way, leaving his dog in her carrier fastened to the back of his rig.

"I was driving by and saw two buggies parked by your daed's barn, so I decided to stop and give you my news." Henry's smile stretched wide.

"What news is that?" Elsie asked.

"I've hired a driver, and me and Peaches will be heading to Florida next week."

"So you're really going to do it, huh?" Elsie remembered hearing Henry previously mention his desire to go there.

He bobbed his head enthusiastically. "I've rented a small house in Pinecraft, and I plan to stay through the winter. Won't return to Ohio till the weather warms up." Henry stared at the ground and shuffled his feet. "I'd hoped your daed could make a trip to Florida with me, but since that's not gonna happen, at least I'll have my *hund* to keep me company."

"It sounds like a real adventure." Arlene smiled. "Someday, when Samuel's older, maybe my family will make it to Florida. I'm sure the kinner would love being able to run around in the sand and play in the waves."

Elsie thought about Doris, and

how she and Brian had talked about going to Sarasota for a vacation. Once Doris's leg healed, it might do her some good to get away for a while — especially to someplace warm.

"I'm surprised to see you two here today," Henry commented. "I heard what happened to Doris and figured you'd be in Berlin taking care of her."

"We've been doing that," Elsie replied. "But Aunt Verna showed up yesterday to help out, so Arlene and I decided to take off for a few hours and get some more sorting done."

"Any luck finding your daed's will?"

Arlene shook her head. "It's like

looking for a sewing needle in a bale of hay."

Henry laughed. "There's an awful lot here for you to go through. My good friend was quite the hoarder."

"How well we know," Elsie and Arlene said at the same time.

"Well, I won't keep ya. If I don't get goin' soon, Peaches will probably wake up and start howling."

Elsie leaned closer to Arlene and whispered in her ear. When her sister nodded, she stepped up to Henry and said, "Ben Yoder came by earlier, with a pheasant he'd stuffed for Dad. How would you like to have it, in remembrance of him?"

"Are you sure? You already gave

me his old straw *hut.*"

"The hat won't hold up forever," Arlene said, "but you can put the pheasant somewhere in your house, and it should last a long time."

"Jah, probably a lot longer than me." Henry's eyes misted and he gave them both a hug. "I'd be happy to take the pheasant. Oh, and when I get to Florida, I'll remember to send you both a postcard."

Berlin

"What would you like for supper this evening?" Aunt Verna asked when she entered the living room.

Doris turned the corner of the page down from the book she was reading. "I believe there's a package of ground beef in the refrigerator. Maybe you could make a meatloaf."

The older woman's gray eyebrows squished together. "You want me to fix ground peas?"

Exasperated, Doris heaved a sigh. For most of the day, her aunt had misinterpreted what she'd said. *Her hearing is probably getting worse. It would make things easier if she would get a hearing aid.* "Aunt Verna," Doris said loudly and as patiently as she could, "I suggested that you make a meatloaf for supper, using the ground beef in the refrigerator."

Aunt Verna moved her head slowly up and down. "Sure, I can do that. Should I get started on it now?"

"If you like." Doris made sure to speak loud enough. She felt worn out from repeating herself so many times throughout the day.

"All right then. Give a holler if you need anything." Aunt Verna turned and shuffled off toward the kitchen.

Even though Doris appreciated the extra help, she'd rather it be one of her sisters doing the cooking and cleaning for her. In addition to Aunt Verna's inability to hear things well, she often became sidetracked, like when she'd left the refrigerator door open after lunch. Doris discovered it when she'd hobbled out to the kitchen for a glass of water. Fortunately, she had caught it before anything spoiled.

Another time, Aunt Verna turned on the water in the kitchen sink and forgot to turn it off because she'd gone outside to fill the birdfeeders. Doris heard it running all the way from the living room.

She shut the book, placing it on her lap, and closed her eyes. *I wouldn't even be in this predicament right now if I hadn't fallen down the stairs.* Tears seeped from her eyes. *I can't do much of anything around the house. I have to rely on others to help me. Their support is appreciated, but I feel helpless and don't like being this way.* She sniffed and wiped the tears from her cheeks. *My clumsiness caused me to lose the child I so desperately wanted.*

Opening her eyes, Doris placed both hands on her stomach. "I'm sorry, so sorry," she sobbed. Even though the baby was gone, she spoke as though it was still there. "This is all my fault. I'm the reason you were never born."

Doris rubbed her nose, breathing slowly to calm herself. *Will I ever conceive again?*

CHAPTER 6

Charm

"There's a postcard and a couple of bills lying on the table. I went out and got them when the mail came earlier." Aunt Verna unwrapped a piece of peppermint candy and popped it in her mouth.

"Who's the postcard from?" Elsie questioned.

"Go ahead — take a look."

Elsie picked up the card and smiled. "It's from Dad's friend Henry Raber. He says he and

Peaches are doing well, and enjoying the warm weather in Sarasota. They've been going to the beach quite a bit, and Henry often visits with other snowbirds staying in Pinecraft." Elsie placed the card back on the table. "I'm glad he was able to make this trip. It's hard to believe he's been there a week and a half already."

"Jah. Henry's a nice man, and I'm sure he's been lonely since your daed passed on. I'm glad he's having a good time down there." Aunt Verna crunched on her candy.

Elsie picked up the bills, setting them on her dad's rolltop desk to pay.

"You know, Elsie, I still don't understand why you want me to stay here." Aunt Verna put both hands on her hips and frowned, her upbeat countenance suddenly changing. "I was perfectly happy helping out at Doris's. Besides, I thought you and Arlene wanted to search for your daed's will."

"We do, but we thought it would be better if you were helping us since you said previously that Dad told you where he'd put the will." Elsie made sure her explanation was loud enough for her aunt to hear. "Arlene and I will take turns helping out at Doris's, while the other one is here sorting things with you."

"Guess that makes sense, but as I've said, I don't remember where my bruder said he put it." Aunt

Verna took a seat at the table and massaged her forehead. "That's the problem with getting older. You lose your thinker, and your ears don't work so good anymore. Makes me feel *nixnutzich* sometimes."

Elsie patted her aunt's shoulder. "You're not worthless. I appreciate you staying here and helping me sort things." She gestured to the refrigerator. "In addition to doing more sorting, I'd like to clean that, inside and out, as well as defrost the freezer section. The last time I put something in there for Glen, I noticed it was thick with ice."

"I could bake some peanut butter *kichlin* while you're doing that. I'll bet Glen would enjoy having some when he gets home from work this evening."

Elsie smiled. "I know he would. Peanut butter is my eldest son's favorite kind of cookie. After we're done in the kitchen we can do more sorting and searching."

Aunt Verna tipped her head. "What did you say?"

Elsie repeated herself.

"Oh, okay. I'll get started on the kichlin right away."

While Aunt Verna got out the baking supplies, Elsie set a pan of warm water in the freezer, hoping the ice would thaw while she cleaned the inside of the refrigerator.

By the time the first batch of cookies had been taken from the oven, the ice in the freezer had melted enough so Elsie could begin chipping away what was left. Removing a bag of frozen peas, she was surprised to discover a gallon-size plastic bag behind it. At first, she thought it was empty, but on closer look, she realized there was large manila envelope inside. "How strange. I wonder what this could be."

Elsie opened the plastic bag and took out the envelope. After reading the words on the outside, written in black marking pen, she gasped. "It's Dad's will! I've found the will!"

Aunt Verna dropped her spatula on the counter and hurried over. "Did you say you found your daed's will?"

"Jah."

"Where was it?"

"In there." Elsie pointed to the freezer section. "It was behind a package of frozen peas."

Aunt Verna stood several seconds, blinking her eyes rapidly. Suddenly, her mouth opened wide and she screeched. *"Ach,* my! I remember now. How could I have been so *schlappich?"*

Elsie's forehead wrinkled. "What do you mean? How were you careless?"

Aunt Verna took a seat at the table and motioned for Elsie to do the same. "This is so unbelievable, I barely believe it myself."

Desperate to know more, Elsie

clutched her aunt's arm. "Do you know why Dad's will was in the freezer? Did he put it there?"

"No, he did not." Aunt Verna's cheeks reddened. "I remember it all now, as though it happened yesterday." She sucked in a quick breath and continued. "When your daed told me he'd made out a will and had it notarized, he took it out of the rolltop desk. Then he showed me the manila envelope, which he kept in a plastic bag, so if something were spilled on it, no harm would be done." She paused and drew in another breath. "About that time, we heard a commotion going on outside with the horses. So Eustace handed me the bag and asked if I'd put the will back in the desk."

"But it wasn't in the desk, Aunt Verna. Arlene and I looked through every drawer and cubby."

"That's because it was in the freezer."

"But how'd it get there?"

"I don't actually remember doing it." Aunt Verna glanced around, as though searching for answers. "I realize now how it must have happened. I had a bag of peas in one hand, and the will in the other. I must have put them both in the freezer by mistake." She paused, rubbing her chin. "Then, anxious to know what was going on with the horses, I hurried outside and forgot that your daed had asked me to put the will away in his desk."

Elsie sat in stunned silence. The freezer was the last place she would have thought to look for Dad's will. Now that it had been found, she needed to notify her siblings and call everyone together so the will could be read.

Akron

Joel was about to stop working for the day when his cell phone rang. Seeing it was Elsie, he answered the call.

"Hi, Joel. I'm calling to let you know Dad's will's been found."

Joel released a throaty laugh. "Well, hallelujah! It's about time! Where'd ya find it?"

"In Dad's freezer."

His head jerked back. "Say what?"

"It was inside a plastic bag behind some frozen peas."

"I knew our dad was eccentric, but what in the world was he thinking, putting the will in the freezer? How did he think we'd ever find it there?"

Elsie cleared her throat. "Actually, it was Aunt Verna who put the will in the freezer, but she did it without thinking."

"I would say so. No one with half a brain would do something that stupid on purpose." Joel's face heated. "I — I didn't mean she was stupid. It just doesn't make sense that she would put Dad's will in the freezer."

"Dad had shown her the document, and when he went outside to check on the horses, Aunt Verna got sidetracked and accidently put it in the freezer along with the bag of peas." Elsie paused. "Would you be able to meet with us tomorrow evening for the reading of the will?"

"Why wait that long? I'm free tonight. Can't we do it then?"

"It wouldn't give me time to notify everyone and make plans to get together. I'll speak to Arlene and Doris, then call you as soon as we have a definite time and place."

"Okay, whatever." Joel released a noisy breath. *I should realize by now that we're operating on Amish time, not mine.*

Berlin
Joel's heart pounded as he neared

Doris's house. He had been counting the minutes all day, anxious to get here this evening for the reading of Dad's will. He'd had a hard time sleeping last night, wondering what his share of the inheritance would be. The only thing that helped him get through this day was keeping busy on the job he'd begun yesterday.

When Joel started up his sister's driveway, he spotted three buggies parked near the barn. *I wonder who else is here besides Arlene and Elsie. Sure hope they didn't invite anyone outside the family to join us. This is no one's business but ours.*

He turned off the car and got out. Taking the steps two at a time, Joel knocked on the door. He was greeted by Brian, who invited him in. "Everyone's in the living room waiting for you."

Joel removed his jacket and hung it on a wall peg, then followed Brian into the next room. Doris sat in the recliner with her leg propped up, while Elsie, John, Arlene, and Larry were seated on the couch. Joel spotted Aunt Verna in the rocking chair. "Are you here for the reading of Dad's will?"

She tilted her head. "Excuse me. What was that?"

Joel repeated his question.

"Jah. Glen brought me over tonight. He's in the kitchen, eating a snack."

"Speaking of the will, where is it?" Joel asked.

"Right here." John held up a large manila envelope and stood. "Your sisters asked if I would read it." He motioned to the couch. "So you can take my seat there, if you like."

"Oh, okay." Joel took a seat beside Elsie and put both hands on his knees to keep his feet from tapping the floor. He couldn't remember the last time he'd felt so anxious.

"Would anyone like a cup of coffee before we get started?" Elsie asked. "I made a fresh pot a while ago."

"No, I'm good. Let's get on with it, shall we?" Joel's neck and shoulders tensed as he leaned slightly forward.

John opened the envelope and pulled out four smaller envelopes, along with a folded document. He placed the envelopes on the coffee table, unfolded the will, and began. "I, Eustace J. Byler, being of legal age and sound mind, do declare that this is my last will and testament. I hereby revoke, annul, and cancel all wills and codicils previously made by me, either jointly or separately. This last will expresses my wishes without undue influence or duress."

John paused and cleared his throat. Continuing to read the will, he stated the names of each of Eustace's children and their dates of birth. "I also appoint my sister, Verna Weaver, as the person responsible to ensure that this will is followed. Should she precede me in death, I appoint my son-in-law, John Troyer.

"The envelopes provided with this will for my children stipulate what each of them will receive. However, they are not to be opened until such time as my son, Joel Byler, performs a heartfelt, selfless act. The selfless act must be voted upon by all three sisters, with the final decision being made by Verna as to whether the stipulation has been met."

Heart thumping so hard he felt it might explode in his chest, Joel leaped to his feet. "That's not fair! How come Dad picked on me?" His hand shook as he pointed at all three of his sisters. "Why didn't Dad ask each of you to do something selfless? How come I have to jump through hoops in order to get my inheritance?"

"It's not only you, Joel," Elsie spoke up. "We all have to wait to open our envelopes until you've done a selfless act that's agreed upon by each of us."

Joel didn't understand how his oldest sister could sit there with such a calm look on her face. "What about you, Doris? How do you feel about this?"

"It doesn't matter how I feel. We have to abide by Dad's wishes," she responded.

Arlene nodded. "He must have had a reason for the four envelopes with our names on them, as well as the request he made of you."

Anger bubbled within Joel as he folded his arms and glared at the piece of paper in John's hands. Then he looked at Aunt Verna. She'd started rocking her chair really fast. "Did you know about this beforehand? Did Dad tell you what he was going to do?"

She looked at him strangely, while tipping her head. "Do about what?"

Joel clapped his hands together so hard, Aunt Verna nearly jumped out of her chair. "Didn't you hear a word John read?"

"Of course I did. He spoke plenty loud enough for me to hear." She left her seat and walked up to Joel. "My bruder wanted you, his only son, to do something meaningful for someone other than yourself."

Joel looked down at the envelopes lying on the coffee table. He was tempted to grab his and open it right now.

Aunt Verna touched Joel's arm. "Before your daed died, he and I talked quite a bit about you."

"Is that so? I'm sure whatever he had to say was negative."

Tears welled in her eyes. "Your selfish actions hurt him, Joel. I'm sure many of the things you've said and done have hurt your sisters, too."

Joel didn't bother to look at Doris, Elsie, or Arlene. He already knew what they thought of him.

"You need to give this some serious thought," Aunt Verna continued. "If you don't do as your daed said, then none of you will get your inheritance."

"Oh, really? Who's gonna get it then? You? Old Henry?" Joel's voice rose even louder. "Or maybe all Dad's money will go to those horses no one wants to sell." Joel stomped across the room, grabbed his jacket, and stormed out the door. *If Dad thought he was going to make me knuckle under and do whatever he said in order to get my share of his money, he was sorely mistaken. I'm gonna get what's coming to me, but it won't be the way he planned.*

CHAPTER 7

Thursday morning of the following week, Doris sat at her kitchen table with Brian, drinking coffee while they waited for Arlene to arrive. Elsie had gone to Dad's house again, but this time she and Aunt Verna would be going through more magazines, catalogs, and newspapers in case they held money. Once they were done for the day, Elsie planned to do some Christmas shopping at a few stores in Charm and would take Aunt

Verna along.

Doris added some cream and sugar to her coffee, swirling it together with her spoon, then leaned back in her chair. "Arlene said she'd be bringing some of her homemade cinnamon rolls with extra cream cheese frosting."

"That would be nice." Brian smacked his lips before sipping some coffee.

She stared out the window at the birdhouse that was once in her dad's tree house. The last few months had been depressing. It was hard losing Dad, and now trying to get through the loss of her baby.

I don't feel like celebrating Christmas this year, much less buying any presents, Doris thought. *Brian and*

I were so happy about my pregnancy. I wish we could skip Christmas and start the new year. She swallowed some coffee and winced when it burned her throat.

"Are you all right, Doris?" Brian touched her arm. "Does your leg hurt this morning?"

"It's not my leg. It's my throat. I added a little cream to my coffee, thinking it would cool off a bit, but the coffee was still quite hot when I swallowed it."

"Would you like a glass of cold water?" He started to rise from his chair.

"No, I'm okay." She glanced at the clock on the wall. "I don't want you to be late for work, so if you'd like to go now, I'll be fine until

Arlene gets here."

He shook his head. "It's not that late. I can wait awhile longer."

Sighing, Doris drummed her fingers on the table. She wished she could clean her own house, or even go back to work so she could help with the hospital bills that would need to be paid. She had so much time to sit and think. Feeling melancholy wasn't making things better for them.

"Is something bothering you?"

"Jah. I've been thinking more about the stipulations of Dad's will. We have my hospital bill to pay, so we could sure use some extra money."

"True."

"It's not likely any of us will get

our inheritance. What are the chances of Joel completing a selfless act?" Her forehead tightened as she frowned. "I can't imagine what our daed was thinking when he put that clause in his will."

Brian clasped Doris's hand. "I don't know, either, but I do know if we put our trust in the Lord, He will provide for our needs."

Akron

Joel pounded his truck's steering wheel in frustration. He'd taken time off from his job to contact a lawyer about Dad's will, only to learn that his chances of contesting it were slim to none. Since the document had been notarized, with two witnesses present, it would be next to impossible to prove his father was incompetent when he'd made out the will. As far as the stipulation went, the lawyer said Joel's dad had been within his legal rights to disperse his assets as he saw fit. "Besides," he'd added before Joel left his office, "the Amish are inclined to do things a bit differently than we would."

"Yeah, well my dad liked to do everything different," Joel muttered as he sat in the parking lot of the lawyer's office, staring out the window while mulling things over. *Just what kind of a good deed am I supposed to do? I can't imagine what so-called selfless act would meet with my sisters' and Aunt Verna's approval. What in the world was Dad thinking? Did he do this on purpose to get even with me for leaving the Amish faith? Or was it because he didn't like me coming to him a few times and asking to borrow money?*

Joel sagged in his seat, rocking back and forth. *If I didn't need money so bad, I'd walk away from this and let my sisters have everything.* He frowned as the truth of the situation fully set in. If he walked away and refused to comply with his father's wishes, then Elsie, Arlene, and Doris wouldn't get their share of the inheritance, either. It was a catch-22. He needed to talk to someone about this — someone who could help him sort things out and come up with a deed his sisters and Aunt Verna would agree was a selfless act. If he could do that, they would all get their money, and everyone would be happy.

Joel reached into his pocket and pulled out his phone. He'd try calling Tom first; maybe he'd have some good advice. If not, then he might try Kristi.

Charm

"You seem quiet today," Aunt Verna commented as she and Elsie sat at the Chalet in the Valley restaurant, having lunch. "Are you *umgerennt* about your daed's will?"

"I'll admit I'm upset. It's an impossible situation."

"In Luke 18:27, Jesus said, 'The

138

things which are impossible with men are possible with God.' " Aunt Verna placed her hand on Elsie's arm and gave it a few gentle pats. "You must have the faith to believe your bruder can change and become the man your daed wanted him to be."

Elsie sighed, toying with the napkin in front of her. "We all want Joel to change, but unless he gets right with God, he will never set his selfish desires aside and learn to truly care about others." She picked up her cup of tea and took a drink. "My other concern is that one of my sisters, or even me, will become so desperate for money we'll accept whatever deed Joel may decide to do as good enough, just so we can get our share of the inheritance."

"That will not happen because I will have the final word as to whether he has actually done a heartfelt, selfless act. Now let's commit this situation to God and enjoy the rest of our lunch." Aunt Verna smiled. "This meal is on me."

Elsie knew better than to argue. Her aunt was strong-willed, just like Dad. When she made up her mind on something, it was best to let it stand. She only hoped Joel would come to his senses and do a good deed they could all agree upon.

Akron

Kristi sat beside Audrey's bed, silently praying while she held the elderly woman's hand. Audrey was going downhill so fast and was often unresponsive. It broke Kristi's heart when she thought how sad it was that no one other than herself and the other staff members visited Audrey.

Last week, knowing how much her patient loved flowers, Kristi had bought a Christmas cactus in full bloom and placed it on the table beside Audrey's bed. "Thank you," Audrey had whispered tearfully. "You're an angel, Miss Kristi."

Kristi would make sure to water the cactus as needed and hoped it would continue to bloom all the way past Christmas.

Audrey's eyes opened, and she offered Kristi a weak smile. "Oh, it's you — my angel of mercy. How long have you been sitting here?"

Kristi glanced at her watch. "Fifteen minutes or so. I haven't said anything because I didn't want to wake you."

Audrey lifted a shaky hand, letting it fall close to the edge of her bed. "You spend too much time with me. Don't you have other patients to tend to?"

"Yes, I do, and they are all taken care of." Kristi took Audrey's hand, holding it gently. "You slept most of the morning, and I've been worried about you."

"I'll be going home soon, and

then you won't have to worry anymore," Audrey murmured. "I will be safe in the arms of my Lord."

In an attempt to hold back tears, Kristi pointed to the cactus. "It's doing well. I think it likes it here in your room."

Audrey gave a feeble nod. "I believe there will be lots of flowers in heaven."

Kristi swallowed hard, barely able to speak around the lump in her throat. "According to what I read in the Bible, there will be lots of beautiful things in heaven for us to enjoy."

"Yes." Audrey's eyelids closed, and Kristi could tell from her steady breathing that she had fallen asleep.

Slipping quietly from the room, she started down the hall. When she entered the break room a few minutes later, her cell phone vibrated in her pocket. She pulled it out to see who was calling. It was Joel, so she let it go to voice mail, as she had done since their breakup.

"How's Audrey?" Dorine asked, joining Kristi for their afternoon break.

"Not well. She's failing fast, but she did wake up and talk to me for a few minutes."

Dorine fixed herself a cup of coffee. "Audrey's your favorite patient here, isn't she?"

"It's not that she's my favorite, exactly, but she definitely needs me the most, and not just in a physical sense."

"I understand what you're saying. The poor woman has no family to sit beside her bed and offer comfort. You've done that for her, Kristi. And the cactus you bought is proof of how much you care."

"Audrey's a special lady, and she's ministered to me along the way, too." Kristi took an orange from the fruit bowl on the table and sat down. Before peeling it, she glanced at her cell phone and decided to listen to the message Joel had obviously left.

"Hey, Kristi, this is Joel. I hope you're doing well." There was a short pause. "I'm faced with an unusual situation right now and could really use some advice." Another pause — this one followed by a groan. "The thing is, my dad's will was finally located — in his freezer of all places. But I don't know how much my share of the inheritance is because Dad wrote a ridiculous stipulation. He expects me to do some kind of a good deed — he called it a selfless act. And until I do it and it's accepted by my sisters, as well as my aunt, neither me nor my siblings can open the envelopes he left us, which will let us know how much we are entitled to. So what I need to know is what kind of good deed would be considered a selfless act. Since you've done many good deeds working as a nurse, I figured you'd be the one to ask. When you get this message, I'd appreciate it if you'd give me a call."

Kristi sat, staring at her phone, trying to process all Joel had said. Could it be true, or was it just another attempt to get her to call so he could try to convince her to take him back?

If it is true, she thought, *Joel's father made a wise decision, for Joel surely needs to think of someone other than himself for a change. But if he does a good deed only to get the money he wants so badly, then nothing will have been gained.*

Kristi hoped for Joel's sake, as well as for his family, that he would come to realize the importance of putting other people's needs ahead of his own. But in order to do a true selfless act, he would need to first get right with God.

CHAPTER 8

Farmerstown, Ohio

Joel had spent the last few days wracking his brain, trying to come up with something he could do to earn the right to open the envelope Dad left for him. This morning he'd come up with a plan, and as soon as he finished working for the day, he headed to the schoolhouse where Anna taught. Hopefully the scholars would be gone by the time he arrived. If things were as they had been when he was in school, the teacher would still be there.

When Joel pulled his truck into the schoolyard, he saw a few children milling about. It was a good indication that they'd been dismissed for the day. He popped a breath mint in his mouth and got out of the truck. As he walked toward the door, his nephew Scott stepped out, carrying a lunch box in one hand while adjusting his straw hat with the other.

"Hey, Uncle Joel! What are you doin' here?" Eyes wide, the boy looked up at Joel and grinned.

Joel raked his fingers through the back of his hair. "I . . . umm . . . came by to talk to your teacher."

Scott tipped his head, looking quizzically at Joel.

"It's just a little grown-up talk." No way was Joel about to explain the reason for his visit with Anna.

"Are ya comin' to the school Christmas program tomorrow evening? Me, my brother, and my sisters all have parts." The boy moved his head slowly up and down. "We've been practicin' for the last couple of weeks."

"I bet you have." Joel remembered how excited he used to get when he was a boy and the class would prepare for the program their parents and other family members would be invited to attend. He'd always tried to do his best so he wouldn't embarrass his folks.

Joel flinched when he thought about Christmas, only a few days away. He'd been invited to spend Christmas Eve with his buddy, Tom, but Christmas Day he would be by himself. He'd thought maybe one of his sisters would invite him to spend the holiday at her house, but after the scene he'd created when Dad's will was read, he wasn't surprised no one had asked. *I wonder what Kristi will be doing this year. I sure miss spending time with her. It seems odd not to have bought her a gift.* Joel was giving in to self-pity, but he couldn't seem to help himself. He felt like a ship without an anchor these days.

"So are ya comin' to the Christmas program?" Scott tugged on Joel's jacket.

"Maybe. If I get off work in time

to drive down here."

"Sure hope you can make it." The boy continued to look at Joel. "Guess I'd better head out. Doug, Martha, and Lillian went home already. I stayed after to practice my part a bit longer."

Joel gave Scott's shoulder a squeeze. "I'll try to be there to see you perform."

"Okay! See you soon, Uncle Joel."

Joel watched his nephew head out on his bike, then turned and went into the schoolhouse. He found Anna at the front of the room, sitting behind her desk and going over paperwork. When Joel cleared his throat, she jumped.

"I — I'm surprised to see you, Joel. If you stopped by to see one of your nieces or nephews, they've already left." Anna's cheeks were bright pink, and her blue eyes as vivid as ever.

"Well, I . . . uh . . . was visiting with my nephew Scott outside, and he mentioned the Christmas program tomorrow evening. I told him I'd try to make it to the holiday performance, but I actually came here today to see you."

"Oh, what about?" Anna placed her pen beside the papers on her desk.

Joel leaned on her desk, hoping he wouldn't lose his nerve and would be able to say the right words. "See . . . the thing is . . . I came to apologize."

Fingering her paperwork, Anna

murmured, "For what, Joel?"

"For hurting you when I broke things off and left the Amish faith." There, it was out. If she accepted his apology he'd stop by Dad's place and tell Aunt Verna what he'd done. Telling Anna he was sorry would surely be considered a self-less act.

She blinked a couple of times, and the color in her cheeks darkened. "What brought this on all of a sudden? Have you changed your mind about being English?"

He shook his head. "I'm happy living with modern things. I . . . I've been thinking about us, though, and wanted you to know that I feel bad about the way things ended." Joel leaned a bit closer.

"Will you accept my apology?" Remembering how his dimpled smile used to temper Anna's mood whenever they got into a disagreement in the past, Joel thought he'd go that route and see if it would work on her now. So he gave Anna his deepest smile, gazing into her eyes. Hoping to ensure success in his endeavor, Joel placed his hand on hers and gave her fingers a tender squeeze.

Blushing further, Anna gave a slow nod. "I . . . I appreciate you coming by. It means a lot to me."

"Good." He moved away from her, shuffling his feet and feeling a bit guilty for coming here with an ulterior motive. He hoped she hadn't gotten the wrong impression.

Joel hadn't actually lied to Anna; he did feel bad for hurting her in the past. But if not for the stipulation in Dad's will, he probably never would have apologized.

"Guess I'd better go and let you get back to whatever you were doing. See you around, Anna." Joel turned from the desk.

"Remember, if you're not doing anything tomorrow evening, you're welcome to come to our Christmas program," Anna called sweetly.

He lifted his hand in a parting wave. "I will try to be there." *I'll only be coming for Scott.*

Charm

Feeling rather pleased with himself,

Joel whistled a tune he'd learned as a boy and turned onto the road leading to Dad's place. He felt good about his visit with Anna and was confident that when he told Aunt Verna, she'd be impressed. If she agreed what he'd done met the condition of the will, then surely his sisters would, too. Since Anna was Doris's friend, Doris would no doubt be pleased to learn of Joel's apology.

As Joel sat in his truck on the hill above Dad's house, he was tempted to get out and wander around, reflecting on his childhood a bit. He could sit on his old rock-seat and daydream awhile, but it was really too cold for that. Besides, Joel was anxious to speak with his aunt.

Turning the steering wheel, he drove down the driveway and parked his vehicle near the barn. When he stepped out and heard the horses whinny, he was tempted to lead them into the barn, as he'd done for a good many years while growing up. But it wasn't his job anymore. Glen was staying here, and he'd take care of the animals when he got home from work, if he wasn't here already.

Shaking his thoughts aside, Joel hurried up the front porch and knocked on the door. He waited several seconds, and when no one answered, he knocked again, a little louder this time. If Aunt Verna was here, she may not have heard him.

A few more seconds passed. Joel was about to try the door when it suddenly swung open. Aunt Verna, wearing a black scarf on her head, looked at him quizzically. "This is an unexpected surprise. Have you been working in the area today?"

"No, I . . ." Joel paused and moistened his lips. "Is it all right if I come in?"

She cupped her hand around one ear. "What was that?"

Joel repeated himself, a little louder this time.

"Of course you may." She opened the door wider, and Joel stepped inside. "Should we go in the kitchen? I was about to fix myself a glass of buttermilk. Would you like some?"

His lips puckered, thinking about the soured milk his dad used to drink. Apparently Aunt Verna liked it, too. "No thanks. I'll take a glass of water, though."

"No problem."

He followed her to the kitchen and took two glasses from the cupboard. After handing one to her, he filled his glass with water and took a seat at the table. Once Aunt Verna had her buttermilk, she joined him. "To what do I owe the pleasure of your visit?" she asked.

Joel took a quick drink and set his glass on the table. "I just came from the schoolhouse in Farmerstown."

"Oh? Did you see your nieces and nephews there?"

"I talked to Scott for a few minutes, but I didn't see the others. I went there to speak with their teacher, Anna Detweiler."

Aunt Verna peered at Joel over the top of her glasses. "Are you two getting back together?"

Joel shook his head. "I went there to tell Anna I was sorry for the hurt I caused when I broke up with her seven years ago."

"Could you repeat that, please?"

"I went there to tell Anna I was sorry for the hurt I caused when I broke up with her seven years ago."

Aunt Verna took a sip of buttermilk. "Has it really been that long?"

"Yes, but that's not the point."

"What is the point?"

"I apologized, and she forgave me."

"I'm glad to hear that. It's always good when a person realizes they've wronged someone and tries to make amends."

Smiling, Joel sagged in his chair with relief. Once Aunt Verna told Doris, Arlene, and Elsie what he'd done, he felt sure he would soon be opening the envelope Dad left for him.

He took another drink and cleared his throat. "So now that I've done my good deed, will you tell my sisters you approve and allow me to receive my inheritance?"

She pursed her lips, frowning deeply. "Apologizing to Anna was not a selfless act, Joel."

Perplexed and feeling a bit miffed, Joel rapped his knuckles on the table. "Then tell me what specifically I need to do."

"I can't. It's something you must find out for yourself." Aunt Verna left her seat and stepped up to Joel, placing her hand on his heart. "It must come from within. It needs to be heartfelt, not something you do only in the hope of getting your share of my brother's money."

Joel's hands curled into a fist as he inhaled a long breath. This was not going the way he'd planned.

"How is your spiritual life, Joel?" Aunt Verna spoke softly. "Have you prayed about this situation?"

He snorted. "I don't pray about anything anymore."

"Well, maybe it's time you start." She looked at him with squinted eyes.

Feeling uncomfortable, Joel pushed back his chair. "Sorry I bothered you, Aunt Verna. You obviously don't understand."

"I believe I do." She pointed a bony finger at him. "It's you who doesn't understand. Your daed knew that, and he tried to —"

Joel whirled around, turning his back on her. "I don't want to hear anything about my dad. He never treated me well after I left home, and the stupid thing he put in his will only proves he had no love for me!" Without waiting for his aunt's response, he jerked open the back door and dashed outside into the frigid air. He was not going to knuckle under and do a selfless act simply because his dad wanted him to. He would figure out some other way to make his fortune!

CHAPTER 9

Farmerstown

It was hard to believe Christmas was only two days away, but as Doris sat beside Brian at the back of the schoolhouse, the reality sank in. Four of her nephews and nieces took turns reciting their pieces. The story of Jesus' birth had been acted out in a Nativity scene, with Doug and Scott both playing the parts of shepherds, while Martha and Lillian were angels.

Doris was glad she'd felt up to

coming, for she wouldn't have wanted to miss it. Her best friend was a talented teacher and had done a good job with the children in preparation for this evening's program.

Glancing around the room, she noticed several hand-drawn pictures of winter scenes. In addition to those, the scholars had made cutout snowflakes of various sizes and shapes to decorate the walls. It brought back memories from when she was a girl. But seeing the scholars and listening to their recitations was bittersweet. It was a harsh reminder that she might never have any children of her own.

She clutched her shawl around her shoulders. *I wonder if my sisters know how fortunate they are to have been given the chance to be mothers.* Her eyes watered, and she bit the inside of her cheek, hoping the tears wouldn't fall. *There's no point feeling sorry for myself. It won't change a thing. I need to accept what's happened to me and find a new purpose in life.*

Doris glanced at Brian and offered him a brief smile when he clasped her hand. He always seemed to be aware when she needed some reassurance or comfort during times of despair. *I feel blessed,* she thought, *to have found a good husband who loves and cares for me.*

Turning her attention to the front of the room, Doris couldn't help but smile when one of the smaller students recited a poem while holding his hand against his heart: "Christmas comes just once a year; but the love of God is always here."

Another child, holding a wrapped package, added, "Christmas is not about gifts or toys. God sent His Son to earth for moms, dads, girls, and boys."

Doris thought about the trials people sometimes faced and how keeping their focus on God helped them get through even the most difficult times. As the children emphasized through their recitations, poems, and skits, the true meaning of Christmas was God's love for His people.

She closed her eyes and offered a

brief prayer. *Thank You, Lord, for the gift of Your Son. Help me love others as You have loved us.*

"The program went well, don't you think?" Arlene said to Larry as they headed for home in their buggy.

"It sure did, and I'm glad the snow they've been forecasting held off so the roads are clear."

Scott groaned from his seat behind them.

"What's the matter, Son?" Arlene called. "Are you disappointed because your uncle Joel didn't come to the program?"

"It ain't that. I mean isn't. I've got a *bauchweh.* Sure hope I don't throw up."

"Hang on, Scott, we'll be home

soon." Larry bumped Arlene's arm with his elbow. "It's no wonder our boy has a stomachache. Did you see all the popcorn he ate after the program?"

"He had some candy, too," Martha interjected. "Teacher Anna brought some for each of the scholars tonight."

Arlene turned and reached over the seat, patting her son's knee. "You'll feel better once we get home and you can go to bed. I have a homeopathic remedy for tummy aches, and that should help, too."

Scott's only response was a deep moan.

Poor little guy. Everything went so well at the program tonight, Arlene felt bad it had ended on a sour note for Scott.

"It was good to see Doris out tonight," Larry commented.

"Jah. I wasn't sure she'd be up to it, but I'm glad she came. She's been cooped up in the house too much since her accident." Arlene shifted under the blanket covering her lap. "Once she gets her cast off, she should do even better."

By the time they arrived home it had begun to snow, and the storm seemed to be getting stronger as the snow stuck to the ground.

"I'll get the snow shovel out before I come in for the evening, in case we get a good accumulation of this white stuff during the night." Larry pulled the buggy up near the house to let everyone out.

"Yippee! Can we make a big *schneeballe*?" Lillian asked when she jumped down from the buggy.

"No snowballs tonight," Larry said. "It's late and you kinner need to get ready for bed. School's out till after Christmas, so if it keeps snowing, you can all play in it to-morrow."

"I don't wanna play in the snow," Martha said. "It's too *kelt* for me."

"It won't be cold if you put on plenty of clothes." Doug ran ahead of his sisters, while Scott trailed behind.

Arlene could tell her boy wasn't feeling well, because normally Scott would have been excited about the snow.

As Larry helped her out of the

buggy, he leaned close and said, "How about making some hot chocolate with marshmallows after the kinner go to bed? We can sit by the fire and enjoy each other's company for a while."

She smiled. "That sounds nice. I'll take care of making it as soon as the little ones are tucked in."

While Arlene and the children headed inside, Larry led the horse to the barn before he put their buggy away for the night.

After Arlene placed the baby in his crib, she sent Doug, Martha, and Lillian upstairs to wash and get ready for bed. Then she gave Scott a remedy for indigestion and took his temperature. He was running a slight fever, but she didn't think it was anything to worry about. By tomorrow morning he'd probably be his old self again, ready to romp and play in the snow.

Akron

Joel entered his mobile home, slung his jacket over a chair, and glanced at the cell phone, noting it was nine o'clock — too late to head for Farmerstown. The school program had probably been over awhile already. He'd planned on going, but his day had been busy, and he'd worked longer than he expected. To make matters worse, it had started snowing about an hour ago, and the vehicles ahead of him had been crawling along. It didn't help that the snow was coming down heavier and sticking to everything. The temperature had dropped suddenly, and the roads could get slick.

Joel's thoughts went to Kristi. He hoped if she was coming home from work, or was on the road for any other reason, that she'd be careful out there. As Christmas drew near, he found himself missing her more than ever. *Sure wish she would have forgiven me and agreed to start over.*

He reached for the TV remote and found the local weather report to see what the forecast was for their area. Turning up the volume so he could hear it from the kitchen, he made himself a sandwich.

Maybe it's for the best I didn't go

to the program, Joel thought when he returned to the living room with a ham-and-cheese sandwich. *With the tension between me and my sisters, I may have said or done the wrong thing.* Sometimes Joel felt as if his family looked for things they didn't like about him. If his sisters cared about his financial situation, they would have spoken up when John had read the will and admitted that Dad's demands were ridiculous. If they'd all stuck together on this, they could have opened their envelopes by now. But of course, they'd have to get Aunt Verna to agree to it, as well. Joel had always liked and respected his aunt, but sometimes she could be downright stubborn, like his dad.

"She should have accepted my apology to Anna as a selfless act," he mumbled, leaning his head against the back of the couch. "Now I'm stuck trying to figure out what my next move should be."

When Joel had left his dad's place after his conversation with Aunt Verna, he'd decided to stop trying to come up with something everyone would see as heartfelt. But after he'd cooled down, and taken another look at his bank account, along with the few jobs he had lined up for the rest of the month, Joel realized he needed to keep trying to meet the stipulations of the will. There had to be something he could do that wouldn't be a big sacrifice for him but would still satisfy his sisters and Aunt Verna. He needed to figure out what it was.

"I see you're working the evening shift again," Yvonne Patterson, one of the other nurses, said when she passed Kristi in the hall. "Are you filling in for Barbara?"

Kristi turned to face Yvonne. "Yes. Shortly before I was supposed to get off work, our supervisor let me know Barbara had called in sick. I volunteered to take her place."

"How come? I would think you'd be exhausted after working all day."

"I'll admit it's not easy working back-to-back shifts, but as the week's progressed, Audrey's gotten worse, and I wanted to be with her tonight." Kristi sighed. "She hardly recognizes me anymore, but I keep hoping she'll rally a bit."

Yvonne gave Kristi's arm a gentle pat. "You have a genuine heart for your patients, and everyone here speaks highly of you. I've heard some folks call you a saint."

Kristi felt the heat of a blush erupt on her cheeks. "I'm definitely not that. I just try to treat everyone kindly and do what the Bible says."

"Your Christianity shows. You don't talk about it all over the place. You live it."

Kristi and Yvonne visited a few more minutes, then moved down the hall to check on patients. Unexpectedly, an image of Joel flashed across Kristi's mind. *I think I may have failed at being a Christian example to him,* she thought with regret. *If I'd been more Christ-like, maybe he would have turned his life over to the Lord instead of putting himself first.*

I shouldn't be thinking about this right now, she told herself. *I can't undo the past, nor can I, or anyone else, make Joel become a Christian if he doesn't want to. He was raised in a Christian home and exposed to Bible teaching from the time he was a boy. Joel became selfish and self-centered of his own accord. All I can do is pray for him — pray that he will see the truth before it's too late.*

Pushing her thoughts aside, Kristi stepped into Audrey's room. The light beside her bed was still on, and Audrey's eyes were open. For a minute, Kristi thought the dear woman was staring at the ceiling, but taking a closer look, she realized Audrey wasn't moving.

Kristi's heart pounded as she checked for a pulse. Nothing. And no breath came from Audrey's slightly open mouth.

"You've gone home," Kristi murmured tearfully. "Your body is healed, and now you are in the presence of the Lord."

CHAPTER 10

"I appreciate you having me over this evening." Joel flopped into a chair in Tom's living room. "Otherwise I'd have been alone on Christmas Eve."

Tom's dimples deepened as he took a seat on the couch across from Joel. "You're welcome to stay the night and spend Christmas Day here, too."

"Naw, that's okay. Your folks will be here tomorrow, and I wouldn't feel right about cutting in on your family time."

"It's no big deal. I'm sure Mom and Dad wouldn't be bothered if you joined us for dinner." Tom thumped his stomach. "Mom will be cooking a juicy ham, baked potatoes, and a green bean casserole. My contribution to the meal will be the pumpkin and apple pies I bought at a local bakery the other day."

Tom's offer was tempting, but Joel declined. "My aunt Verna called this morning and invited me to join her at my sister Elsie's place for Christmas dinner. Things have been kind of tense between me and my family since Dad's will was found, so I think I ought to show up and try to be sociable. I'm taking everyone gifts, so maybe they'll see it as a selfless act."

Tom's forehead wrinkled. "You think so?"

"Sure, why not?"

Before Tom could reply, his cell phone rang. "I'd better take this call. It's my mom." He grabbed the phone, lying beside him, and headed out to the kitchen.

Joel leaned back in his chair, closed his eyes, and tried to relax. Tom kept yakking like a magpie, carrying on a lengthy conversation with his mother, while Joel tried to ignore it. He'd told his buddy previously about the situation with his family and Dad's stipulation regarding the will. Now he wondered if he should have kept quiet. From the look on his friend's face before his phone rang, he didn't approve of Joel buying gifts for his family in the hope of getting the envelope Dad had left for him. It didn't matter what Tom thought. Joel had to try something to get his aunt's and sisters' approval.

"I'm sorry our new youth pastor couldn't join us this evening," Kristi's mother said as the three of them sat at the dining-room table, eating open-faced sandwiches and tomato soup. "I've tried on several occasions to schedule a time when he could come for a meal, but either he's been busy or you've had to work." She looked at Kristi with a hopeful expression. "But I'm not giving up. If I can't work something out before the end of the year, I'll try to set something up with Darin for the first or second week of January."

Kristi groaned inwardly. Mom meant well, but Kristi had no interest in developing a new relationship with anyone so soon after breaking up with Joel. While the pain from it was diminishing, at times like tonight, she missed what they'd once had. Then there was the sadness she felt over losing dear, sweet Audrey. A short memorial service would be held at the nursing home the day after Christmas. Since Audrey had no family members, only the staff and some of the patients would attend.

"Are you feeling okay, Kristi?" Dad asked, breaking into her thoughts. "You're not your usual talkative self this evening."

"I was thinking about the patient we lost at the nursing home last night. I'm going to miss my visits with her." Kristi took a bite of her sandwich. The slice of french bread was covered with lettuce, turkey lunchmeat, and Swiss cheese. Squiggles of mustard and mayonnaise traveled across the top. Normally she would have devoured the meal because it tasted so good, but tonight her appetite was diminished.

"Why don't you try to find another nursing job, Kristi?" Mom asked. "Something where you're not working with elderly patients."

"I enjoy my work there. I consider it a type of ministry." Kristi hoped her mother wouldn't go on and on about this. Sometimes Mom offered her opinions too freely, especially where Kristi was concerned.

"So what should we do after we're done eating?" Dad asked. "Should we open our gifts or play a game?"

"We can't open gifts, Paul." Mom nudged Dad's arm. "We've always waited till Christmas morning to do that. And since Kristi will be spending the night here, we can get up early if we want, eat the breakfast casserole I put together earlier today, and then open our Christmas presents to each other."

Leave it up to Mom to make sure

we keep to our tradition. Kristi couldn't help smiling. Some things never changed.

"Okay, then," Dad conceded, "as soon as I'm done eating, I'll get out one of our favorite board games. We can play awhile and then have some hot chocolate and ginger cookies."

Mom swatted his hand playfully. "I'm surprised there are any left. You ate enough of those cookies when I baked them earlier this week."

He reached over and patted her cheek. "I never could resist snitching any of your baked goods. You're the queen of our kitchen."

Mom giggled. "So what does that make you?"

He puffed out his chest, grinning widely. "The king, of course. Whatever you bake, I eat. What a great arrangement."

Kristi loved to see the banter between her parents. They'd been sweethearts in high school and had gotten married soon after graduating from college. It warmed her heart that even after being married nearly thirty years Mom and Dad were still in love and enjoyed each other's company. Kristi hoped to have that kind of a relationship with a man someday.

Farmerstown

"How is Scott feeling?" Aunt Verna asked soon after she, Uncle Lester, and Glen entered Arlene's house.

Arlene's brows raised. "How'd you know he wasn't feeling well? He didn't complain of a bauchweh until we were on our way home from the schoolhouse last night."

"I'm the one who told her." Glen spoke up. "I heard about it from Uncle Larry when I came by here this morning to see if his driver could take me to work." He leaned against the doorframe. "My driver came down with the flu last night and couldn't pick me up."

"I see." Arlene took everyone's coats and hung them up. "I'm glad you made it here today." She gave her uncle a hug.

He smiled, his hazel eyes twinkling. "I wouldn't have missed this special time with our family for all the money in the world."

Arlene invited them into the living room, where Elsie, John, Blaine, and Mary sat, along with Doris and Brian.

Arlene's aunt and uncle took a seat on either side of her. "What about Scott? Is he feeling better today?" Aunt Verna asked.

"Not much, but he doesn't seem to be any worse, either. He's upstairs with Doug, Hope, Lillian, and Martha. I'll call them down as soon as supper is ready to be served."

"And how's this little fellow doing?" Aunt Verna moved over to where Elsie sat, holding Samuel.

"He's been content to have me hold him since we got here fifteen minutes ago." Elsie kissed the top of the baby's head. "I think he loves his aunt Elsie."

John began talking to Lester about how his trip went. Arlene liked to see the family all together. These were the special times that made life worth cherishing.

"While you all visit, I'm going to slip into the kitchen and check on the chicken soup simmering on the stove. Once it's thoroughly heated, we can set out the sandwiches Elsie brought and then call everyone to the table."

"Is there anything I can do to help?" Elsie asked.

"No, that's okay. You're helping by keeping my baby entertained."

Arlene went to the kitchen. When

she lifted the lid on the soup kettle, her mouth watered, and she inhaled deeply. Even when she was a girl, chicken noodle had been her favorite kind of soup. Her children liked it, too — especially Scott. Sometimes when she fixed it, he ate two or three bowls. *I'll bet the delicious aroma of this soup will bring his appetite back tonight.*

A short time later, everyone sat around the table. After their silent prayers, Arlene dished up the soup, and the sandwiches were passed around.

"I'm glad we kept our Christmas Eve meal simple," Elsie said. "Tomorrow at our place, we'll be eating a big meal, so I hope everyone comes hungry to help eat the large turkey John bought the other day."

"I'm looking forward to it." Brian smiled at Doris. "How about you?"

She nodded slowly. "I only wish I could do more to help with the meal."

"It'll be taken care of," Elsie said. "So don't even worry about it."

"Mama, can I be excused?" Scott set his spoon down. "I'm not *hungerich*."

"You need to eat your soup, Son," Larry said. "If you don't, there will be no cookies or candy for dessert."

"I don't care. My belly hurts, and I wanna go lie down."

Arlene looked at Larry, and when he nodded, she said, "Go on up, Scott. I'll check on you in a bit."

Holding his stomach, Scott got

up. Walking slowly, he left the room.

"I'll bet that boy has the flu." Aunt Verna clicked her tongue and nudged her husband's arm. "Sure hope the rest of us aren't exposed to it now."

Glen shrugged his shoulders. "If we are, there's nothing we can do about it. Let's try to enjoy the rest of our meal."

As they continued to eat, the conversation around the table went from talking about the Christmas program at the schoolhouse, to the snowy weather, which had stopped as suddenly as it started.

"Guess we won't get to make any more snowballs." Lillian's chin jutted out. "I only got to make a few this morning before my toes got too cold."

Doug bumped his sister's arm. "That's 'cause ya didn't wear heavy enough socks inside your boots."

Aunt Verna tilted her head in his direction. "Did you say something about a heavy box?"

Uncle Lester looked at her and raised his brows.

The children all snickered, while Doug shook his head. "I said *heavy socks* not *box.*"

"Will Uncle Joel be at your house on Christmas Day?" Martha asked, looking at Elsie.

"I don't know. Aunt Verna invited him to come, but he may have other plans."

"It would be nice if Joel made an

effort to be here to celebrate with the family tomorrow," Uncle Lester said before taking a bite of his sandwich.

"I hope he comes, 'cause if he brings his harmonica, it might make Scott feel better." Martha paused for a drink of water. "He's been wantin' another lesson."

Arlene hoped for her nephew's sake that Joel would join them, too. With it being Christmas, maybe he would be in a good mood. She remembered how much her brother enjoyed Christmas when he was a boy. Of course, they all had, but Joel talked about it nonstop for several days before the big event. Arlene had always thought it was the gifts they received on Christmas morning that Joel liked most of all. He would jump up and down and clap his hands every time someone handed him a gift. Dad used to reprimand him, saying if he didn't calm down, he'd be the last one to get his presents.

After the meal and the dishes were done, the grownups sat at the table playing a new game John had brought along, while the children went back upstairs to play. The game was just getting interesting when Doug bounded down the stairs and raced up to his dad. "Scott's throwin' up, and his belly hurts so bad, he can't even walk."

Concerned, Arlene jumped up. "I think we ought to call one of our drivers and take Scott to the hospital. It may only be the flu, but I'd feel better if he got checked out."

"I agree with you." Larry pushed his chair aside, grabbed his jacket, and went out the door, while Arlene hurried upstairs to check on Scott. This was certainly not the way she'd planned their Christmas Eve gathering to end, but their son's health came first, and she felt sure the others would understand.

Millersburg

"I wish we could have accompanied Larry, Arlene, and Scott to the hospital," Elsie told John as they and their family traveled home by horse and buggy. "I'm anxious to know what they find out and how he's doing."

"They said they would call as soon as they know something." John touched her arm. "I'll go out to the phone shack and check for messages every couple of hours once we get home."

Elsie tried to relax, but she had a horrible feeling something might be seriously wrong with her nephew. It was an inner sense she sometimes got when things weren't as thcy should be. She hoped she was wrong this time, but she would feel much better once they heard something from Arlene.

"It was nice of your aunt and uncle to stay at Arlene's with the kinner," John said.

"Jah. I think Doris and Brian were going to stay awhile longer, too." She sighed deeply. "I believe Doris is doing a little better emotionally, but her old spark isn't back yet."

"It'll come. It's only been a month since she lost the boppli."

"True."

When they rounded the next bend, Elsie spotted flames shooting into the air. With trembling lips, she let out a gasp. "Ach, John! Our house — it's on fire!"

ABOUT THE AUTHORS

New York Times bestselling, award-winning author **Wanda E. Brunstetter** is one of the founders of the Amish fiction genre. Wanda's ancestors were part of the Anabaptist faith, and her novels are based on personal research intended to accurately portray the Amish way of life. Her books are well-read and trusted by many Amish, who credit her for giving readers a deeper understanding of the people and their customs. When Wanda visits her Amish friends, she finds herself drawn to their peaceful lifestyle, sincerity, and close family ties. Wanda enjoys photography, ventriloquism, gardening, bird-watching, beachcombing, and spending time with her family. She and her husband, Richard, have been blessed with two grown children, six grandchildren, and two great-grandchildren.

To learn more about Wanda, visit her website at www.wanda brunstetter.com.

Jean Brunstetter became fascinated with the Amish when she first went to Pennsylvania to visit her father-in-law's family. Since that time, Jean has become friends with several Amish families and enjoys writing about their way of life. She also likes to put some of the simple practices followed by the Amish into her daily routine. Jean lives in Washington State with her husband, Richard Jr., and their three children, but takes every opportunity to visit Amish communities in several states. In addition to writing, Jean enjoys boating, gardening, and spending time on the beach.

The employees of Thorndike Press hope you have enjoyed this Large Print book. All our Thorndike, Wheeler, and Kennebec Large Print titles are designed for easy reading, and all our books are made to last. Other Thorndike Press Large Print books are available at your library, through selected bookstores, or directly from us.

For information about titles, please call:
(800) 223-1244

or visit our Web site at:
http://gale.cengage.com/thorndike

To share your comments, please write:
Publisher
Thorndike Press
10 Water St., Suite 310
Waterville, ME 04901

9-16